Raised-Up Hard i

This book is based on a true story…told to author
by her grandma, Ethel Burgess-Nalley.

Intro…

All my life I have understood to appreciate what I
have…and not focus on 'what I don't have'. This
mindset is largely due to the stories of my
grandma. She also made me see that Christmas
is a time to celebrate the 'Birth of Jesus Christ',
and our families should be celebrating our
'gatherings', not 'gifts'. She taught me to focus on
what I have that 'others' do not—not on what I
'lack'.

Grandma was an amazing survivor. My only regret
is that I did not have the story of her entire
life…just those two, hard years surrounding the
illness and death of her Mama.

Table of Contents

Raised-Up Hard in the

Georgia Pines

Author & Illustrator:
Carol McGinnis-Yeje

Chapter 1:

The Passing

I could not believe this was happening to me. I felt as if it were a dream. I heard all the cries around me—but somehow I could not weep.

This year of 1895, I, Ethel Burgess, 11 years old, was attending my mother's funeral.

The church was packed. Mother's friends and family were many. It was in January. A fresh layer of snow had just fallen. But no one seemed to feel the cold chill.

On the hard, homemade wooden bench of Old Hopewell Church in Milton County, Georgia, I sat with brother Frank (who was 5), sister Lydia (9), and sister Ema (7). Grandpa Bagwell held my baby brother, Roy, who was about 4 months old.

I watched Papa as the tears streamed down his face...and then...I cried. Papa loved Mama. It seemed even harder for him since Mama was only 29 years old.

I watched Grandma and Grandpa Bagwell and wondered how they must feel, seeing their daughter lying there.

As I watched and thought, I realized why Mama had taken so much time to teach me everything a mother does...cause, now I'm the mother...and have been for over two years, ever since Mama got sick.

Oh, how I wish I had not been so busy. How I wish I could have talked with Mama more. How I wish I would have taken more time to show her how much I loved her.

_____

They are opening the casket now. All those feet on that hard wooden floor sound like a slowed-down train, passing through a train station.

I just closed my eyes and remembered how it all began.

Chapter 2:

The Birth of Paul

All of us kids caught the measles. It didn't matter much for us to have 'em, cause kids get over things pretty fast. But what worried Papa was that Mama got the measles, too. And, Mama was in the 'family way'.

So…Mama, being older, had to stay in bed.

"Ethel, get up and cook breakfast," Papa called to me about an hour before sun up. Even though I was just about nine years old, Mama taught me everything to do with cookin'.

So I'd say, "O.K., Papa," and drag out of bed while Lydia (7), Ema (5), and Frank (3) would still be sleepin'.

Papa would light the lamp and set it on the kitchen table and start the fire in the wood stove. I'd put a chair up to the table and get everything ready to make the biscuits.
Then, I'd stand on a stool and 'go at it' with both hands.

When I'd get the ham and eggs cooked, the biscuits would just about be done.

"Go fetch some milk while I wake the younguns'," Papa called out, just as I got breakfast on the table.

I'd run to milk the cow. I'd be back and have the milk strained through a cloth…and in glasses…just about the time they all got to the table.

Papa, William Jackson Burgess by name, would bow his head and pray before we ate. He seemed to cry a little that morning. By the way he kept looking at Mama's chair, I guess it was 'cause he missed her being there.

 Grandma Bagwell came in just as we finished breakfast, "How's Flora this morning, Jackson?" Grandma came to sit with Mama every day since Mama got the measles.

"She didn't sleep too good. I think it's about time for the baby to come," Papa said.

Grandma went in the bedroom with Mama, and I started to follow her. But, Papa said, "Ethel, you wash the dishes. Lydia, Ema, and Frank, go outside and play."

It was times like these that sure made me wish I wasn't the oldest.

While the dish water was warming on the stove, I heard Grandma holler for Papa… "Jackson…it's time! Go get the doc!"

But the doc lived over a mile away. I sure was hope'in' Molly, our mule, wouldn't be stubborn today. As I watched Papa ride off, I peeked into the bedroom.

Poor Mama was hurtin' something awful. Grandma was wipin' the sweat from Mama's face. Then something strange happened. Mama turned cotton white and started holdin' her breath and strained as if she was tryin' to pull Molly to the barn.

All of a sudden Grandma hollered for me to get out of the bedroom—so I ran back in the kitchen—not knowin' what would happen next.

Oh...where is Papa! He should have been here with the doc by now.

The next thing I knew, I heard a cry and I ran to the door of the bedroom. I saw Grandma holdin' our new baby, wrapped in one of Mama's gowns.

Mama was relaxed and smilin' when Papa ran in with the doc.

When Grandma told Papa he had a boy, he started to cry and knelt beside Mama's bed. With his arm around Mama, Papa prayed, "Thank you Lord for this fine boy that you gave us. We'll name him Paul after the great missionary and preacher in the Bible."

And, Papa, Mama, Grandma, and me—hiding behind the door—(and, of course, Paul)…cried.

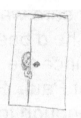

Chapter 3:

Church Night

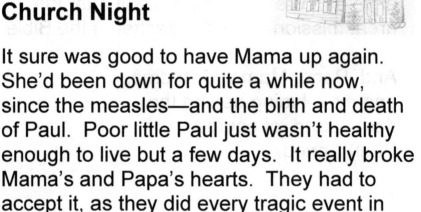

It sure was good to have Mama up again. She'd been down for quite a while now, since the measles—and the birth and death of Paul. Poor little Paul just wasn't healthy enough to live but a few days. It really broke Mama's and Papa's hearts. They had to accept it, as they did every tragic event in our lives.

"Lydia, you help me pick some peas for supper," I yelled on the way down the dusty dirt road to the pea rows.

"I don't have to, and I ain't goin' to!" she shouted, tryin' to get out of work as usual.

"Papa, Lydia won't help me," I whined.

"Get busy, Ethel. Stop complaining. You know we've got to get ready to go to prayer meeting tonight. Get those peas to your mama!"

Well—when Papa spoke, you forgot all about complainin'. So, I scurried down the rows—so as not to get a whippin'.

"Frank, eat with your spoon," Mama scolded at the supper table.

"Yeth, mam," he said, as us girls giggled at his funny talk.

"Eat up, girls. We need to hurry. Ethel, you do your best on the organ tonight." Papa was always wanting me to do my best—so he could brag about my playin'.

Papa would carry our little pump organ on his back to church, which was only a 30-minute walk down the road. I couldn't read music. But just let me hear the tune to one verse and I'd easily play the rest of the song.

_____

"Sweet Hour of Prayer. Sweet Hour of Prayer." You could hear the voices of the people as they sang in the church for a long, long way. They would sing until the sun was almost down and the sky was red like fire.

When I could feel the air coolin' some, and the crickets start to sing along, I could play that organ with my eyes closed. It was like God was breathin' on us—it sure made me feel good.

Singin's over…time for preachin'.

Brother Frank whines for some water. Mama gets the 'mason jar' from under the bench and gives him a drink. Mama always brought a couple of jars of water with us to church.

 "Sit back, Ema," Mama whispered. Ema was always fidgetin' like she had worms.

Papa, who was the church's pastor, kinda' hollered with tears in his eyes, "Jesus is the only way to heaven. He gave His Life on the Cross…so that all who believe 'on' Him, can be 'saved' from 'hell'."

Wow…I sure didn't want to go to hell. I better pray about that. The name of our church was 'Hopewell', and I sure well hoped I would go to heaven.

"Lydia…stop that!" Mama scolded. That Lydia was pullin' splinters off the bench and stickin' 'em straight up—so, if somebody sat down on them, they'd stand up again, right fast. Lydia was always doin' something mean. (It's a good thing Papa sits in the 'Amen Corner' when he's not preachin', with the other men. He would have taken Lydia out of the church and whipped her for sure if he had seen what she'd done this time…)

Everything gets really quiet for the altar call. That's when the sermon is over and the preacher asks if anyone wants to come forward and pray to accept Jesus as their Savior.

"Look, Mama," I pointed. One of the meanest boys at my school started walkin' toward Papa. How he thought Jesus would forgive him all his meanness…I'll never know. But, he sure was cryin'…so, something must've happened to him. I'll know tomorrow at school if he's different or not. _____

On the way home from church I asked Papa if he thought that boy got 'saved' and Papa said, "Be patient, dear Ethel. That's between the boy and the Lord."

Later as we all got ready for bed, and after Papa prayed, me, Ema, and Lydia got in our bed—and Mama, Papa and Frank in the other.

 As I looked out the window at the stars, I wondered how far up Jesus lived, and if He knew I was thinkin' about Him.

Chapter 4:

Last Day of School

"Oh, how I hate to get up in the morning.
But I sure am glad this is the last day of
school." I shouted to Mama.

"Hurry up children," Mama would say in her
sweet soft voice.

Mama was so beautiful. If she had some
fancy clothes and pretty hair combs, she
would sure be the prettiest lady around
these parts.

"Don't forget your ham and biscuits," Mama reminded us.

It's so nice in the morning when spring has set in. All us kids just love goin' barefooted. Except Lydia, of course—her pretty feet are sooooo tender.

"Wait for me," Lydia would whine. I would have to slow down to a creep-walk, waiting on her.

The path through the woods to the old schoolhouse was crooked but fairly level. We would get to a clearin' and it would seem you could just see for miles.

Finally. We would get to the school yard. All shapes and sizes and ages of kids attended. We would run and play until the teacher rang the bell to come inside. Our teacher was a good one. She knew how to handle all of us...no matter how old or big or small.

[Oh, yeah…that mean old boy must have got 'saved'. He sure was acting different…]

"Come on, Lydia. Let's go inside," I would say as I grabbed her arm. This bein' Lydia's first year of school, she sure gave me trouble when I tried to make her sit still durin' class.

"Now, children, I want you all to remember to be here early for the 'spelling bee' tonight. And, remember to bring your 'thinkin' caps'," our teacher said.

Each age group had a review of what they learned during the year. The time would go fast and pretty soon it was time to go home.

Class dismissed! I ran out of the school and continued running until I got to our house. I ran inside and grabbed Mama around her waist, and said, "Oh Mama, I'm so happy. School's out and the 'spelling bee' is tonight!"

Mama just squeezed me a little and said, "You and Lydia must get your chores done."

Then Lydia ran in, sputterin', "Mama, Ethel ran off and left me!"

"Now hush, Lydia. Go wash your hands. Then come back and do some ironing for your Mama," Mama scolded, tenderly.

While I helped Mama finish up dinner, Lydia set the iron on the stove to get it hot. Lydia spread a folded sheet on the table and went to get the gowns that needed ironing. Mama didn't trust her with the dresses, yet. She was a little too young.

We heard Papa comin' up the road with Molly to give her some water while he took time to rest from plantin'.

Lydia started to iron…pushin' back and forth…back and forth. Then, when Lydia started to put the iron back on the stove, somehow she hit the kerosene lamp that was on the table.

BANG! CRASH!

The kerosene lamp hit the floor and made a loud noise. Mama was so scared by the loud noise that she started to scream!

Papa heard Mama scream and ran to the house, just as Mama was about to faint. He helped Mama to bed and stayed with her for a while. He told me and Lydia to get on with our chores and make Ema and Frank stay outside.

Lydia and I cleaned up the broken lamp. She picked up the broken glass. I wet a cloth and wiped up the spilled kerosene from the floor.

Ema and Frank stayed outside, playin' near the big pines. They were playin' church…Frank preached while Ema would 'shout'. They didn't realize what was happenin'. They just played.

It soon began to get dusty-dark. Mama was still in bed. Papa said, "All right now. Let's get ready to go to that 'spellin' bee'."

But, I was thinking about Mama. I asked, "Papa, what about Mama?" Mama had never stayed in bed that long before, except when she had the measles.

"She'll be alright," Papa said. "When we pass Grandma's house on the path, we'll ask her to sit with your Mama until we get home."

So...we all got ready and out the door we ran... skippin' down the path. Frank, runnin' to keep up with Ema, holdin' Papa's hand; Lydia, worryin' about her feet; but...I was worried about Mama.

Chapter 5:

Spring Cleanin' &
Soap Makin'

With school being out, there were hundreds of things to be done. I guess if Mama had to be sick, this was a good time.

I had to take over all the chores, now. I figured cookin' and cleanin' was bad enough. But…I didn't figure on having to do the 'spring cleanin' and makin' soap, too. And, to add to the endless chores, it was 'wheat thrashin' time'. That meant we would have to re-stuff and wash the 'bed-ticks' that we slept on.

"Lydia, you get water and fill the wash pot while I make the fire under it," Papa said.

"Ema, you and Frank play outside. Ethel, you go get a bucket."

Boy, I sure did dread scalding the walls and floors of the house. Mama used to do all the hard work. Now, I have to do it, since I am the oldest.

We would scald the walls each spring—not only to clean the house, but, also to be sure to kill any stray bed bugs and their eggs. Sometimes if the bed bugs settled in during winter, we would scald the walls then, too. If we didn't keep them killed off, they would get in our beds…ouch! They would bite us and it would itch somethin' awful.

"Bring the bucket here, Ethel," Papa said as the water in the wash pot was boiling. Papa would fill the bucket and I would carry it, first, to the sittin' room.

Even though our house had only three rooms, each room was big…and, the walls were high.

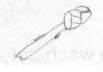 Papa would fix a long tree branch with rags tied around one end. We would dip the rags

in the bucket and start from the top of the walls [standin' in a chair] and scrub from the top to the bottom. Papa would take turns with me, standin' in the chair or scaldin' the bottom of the walls. Since there were spaces between the boards on the walls, part of the outside of the house would be scalded, too.

After the sittin' room, we'd go to the kitchen …always pushin' the furniture to the center of the room. Papa and Lydia would do the movin' while I did the scaldin'.

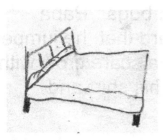

Papa kept the water boilin' in the old black wash pot. As soon as we finished the walls we would take the bed ticks off the beds. After we emptied out the old wheat straw, we put the bed ticks in the pot of scaldin' water.

The bed ticks were made of cloth, sized to fit the beds. They were stitched with extra room to allow lots of wheat straw to make them soft to sleep on. They had an open flap in the middle to make it easy to stuff and then fold over the flap and make some big stitches to hold it all in place.

"Get away from there," Papa shouted. He saw Frank was playin' on the old wheat straw where we dumped it near the pines.

"But we're 'dust' playin' that I'm killed, Papa," Frank stuttered.

"Well, you 'dust' play you're killed somewheres else. That old wheat straw may have some bed bugs," Papa scolded. When Frank heard that, he jumped up and lit out…lookin' like a scare crow with wheat straw comin' out of his shirt and pants.

Papa walked to the edge of the house where we kept our barrel of ashes that we used to make soap. We got the ashes from the fireplace, from the wood we burned durin' the winter. He cut a hole on the bottom of one side of the barrel. Then he took the barrel, placed it on the raised hearth in front of the fireplace. He made a long, small trough-like, funnel and placed it under the hole in the barrel connecting it to a bucket.

 Papa poured water over the ashes and liquid would slowly drift down the trough into the bucket. The liquid that resulted was called 'lye'.

Later that evenin' the 'lye' was ready to put into the wash pot.

"Go get the grease, Ethel, and tell Lydia to come and stir," Papa said.

Papa then put the grease in the pot with the 'lye' and kept it fire-hot. We would take turns stirring until the mixture got thick.

"Ema, you and Frank can help Lydia get the jars out of the storehouse," Papa shouted as Ema and Frank ran to see who would get to the storehouse first.

We would get the jars ready while Papa put out the fire. Then, we would scoop the mixture with a wooden scoop into the jars and let it cool. It always made enough soap to last 'til next spring.

"Mama, I never knew you had to work so hard," I said, kneeling by her bed that night. "It sure is hard doin' all this stuff without you. I guess learnin' to do all this on my own will make me the best wife, ever."

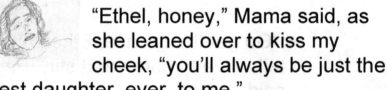 "Ethel, honey," Mama said, as she leaned over to kiss my cheek, "you'll always be just the best daughter, ever, to me."

28

Chapter 6:

The Big White Dog

Summer passed quickly. School starts now in September. I was busy getting Lydia ready for school. Papa said I couldn't go 'cause Mama was too sick and needed me at home.

Grandpa Bagwell came early to help Papa kill the hog. While they were getting everything ready, I continued with my daily chores.

I didn't finish milking the cow that morning. So…I got my milk pail and headed back to the barn. I was milking away when all of a sudden, the cow kicked her foot, hit the pail and milk went all over me.

When I finally got up off the ground and picked up my little tree-legged stool, I saw Frank…near the stall…giggling. I ran to where he was and said, "I guess you really think that's funny. What are you doin' out here, anyway?"

"I 'dust' came out to 'thee' how tuff the cow 'wath'," he said. Then he jumped to run and I saw a sewing needle in his hand. The cow kicked, 'cause, Frank stuck her'.

I walked to the spring to wash the milk off my face. Papa and Grandpa Bagwell had just strung-up the hog with a rope, hanging it on a tree limb.

"You stay here, Ethel, and keep any stray dogs off the hog while the blood drains," Papa said. He gave me a big stick and he and Grandpa starting walking back toward the house.

As I knelt down to wash my face in the spring, I heard something rustling in the bushes. I jumped up and grabbed the stick. I hid behind the tree where the hog was hanging.

Very slowly, and growling in a low tone, a big white dog (that looked like a wolf) came walking by the spring. I was so scared! I didn't think I'd be able to use the stick that Papa gave me even if the white dog tried to eat the hog.

 The big white dog stopped…looked around…and then crossed the spring and continued walking into the woods. I watched until it disappeared into the trees.

Taking a breath, I was then scared again by the sounds of many feet [or paws] headed right for me. I couldn't see anything yet, but

I heard what sounded like a 'cattle-stampede'. As the sounds came closer I could then see men's faces through the bushes.

"Hey…little girl…," one of the men shouted. "Did you see a big white dog come through here?"

"Yes, sir," I said as I stood and shook with terror. "The big white dog crossed the spring right here and headed for those trees."

"Thanks. Now you go tell your Papa that there's a 'mad' dog loose and that he'd better come stand by this hog with his shot gun," the man continued.

I ran to the house and when I reached Papa, I stuttered. I was so scared. "P-Papa, P-Papa, th-those men in the woods were following a b-big wh-white dog that passed right by the hog. They said he was 'mad' and for me to come get you. He said you should stand near the hog with your gun."

"O.K., Ethel…you go get Ema and Frank into the house and check on your Mama. Then run to the school house and tell the teacher about the big white dog. And, you wait for Lydia and walk home with her."

Papa would always buy leather at the slaughter house in Duluth, Georgia, every fall. He'd lay it out on his homemade table in

the

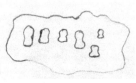

smokehouse. Then he'd cut out our shoes at night by paper patterns he had made of our feet.

As I held the lamp in the smokehouse for Papa to see how to cut shoes that night, I asked, "Papa, what would have happened to me if I'd got bit by that big white dog?"

"Let's just thank the Lord that His Angels were protecting you," Papa said.

When Papa was finished cutting leather for our shoes, he blew out the lamp and took me by the hand as we walked together toward the house. After we went inside, Papa gave me a big hug and said good night.

I knew from the hug that Papa was glad I was not hurt. And I knew the hug meant, "Papa loved me".

Chapter 7:

Lydia's Birthday

Lydia's ninth birthday is a day I'll never forget. It started with a party…

Mama taught me how to make the cake. It looked pretty good…or, at least, I thought so. Frank and Ema just sat around the table, waiting to eat the cake.

I had lots of surprises for Lydia. She was always picking on me and always getting out of chores, which meant more work for me.

Frank would always chase her around the house with live worms. But, I knew Papa wouldn't like it if I brought real worms and put them on the table…so…my first attempt to get even was putting 'paper worms' under

Lydia's plate. I mean they really looked like the real thing.

As Lydia sat down and lifted her plate for me to give her a piece of cake, she saw the 'paper worms' …and she fainted.

 "What happened?" Mama hollered from the bedroom.

"Oh, it's O.K., Mama. Lydia just turned over her chair," I said, which was the truth. She did turn over her chair when she fainted and fell to the floor. "She's not hurt."

Then, me, Ema and Frank dashed a little water on Lydia's face and woke her up. I held her mouth with my hand until she promised not to tell Mama. I told her if she did, Frank would go get the real worms.

Well, Lydia's birthday continued and she never tattled. But I had another surprise planned for bedtime.

We all wash our feet just before getting into bed. This night, I made sure Frank washed first…then Ema…then me…and, finally, Lydia.

When I finished washing, I put 'cockleburs' all around the bottom of the water in the wash-pan. "O.K., Lydia, you can wash your feet now." I was so tickled I could barely breathe.

Lydia sat in the chair, stuck both feet in the water at full force, let out a war-hoop and then, of course... fainted. She was always so scared of  bugs. Anything that felt like 'little feet' on 'her' feet would make her pass-out.

"O.K., Ethel, that's enough. You get in the kitchen and do those dishes," Papa said. "And, stop playing tricks on your sister."

"Aw...hateful on it! Lydia never has to do nothin'!" I murmured.

 About that time I found myself pushed up against the wall with Papa's hand wrapped firmly around my arm. "Ethel...don't you ever let me hear you say such a thing...ever again! Now

wash those dishes!" [Hateful-on-it was considered slang, and not allowed in our home.]

"Yes, sir. I'm sorry, Papa," I whimpered.

I got the pan ready and put the dishes in the pan. As I had my back turned to the stove, Lydia sneaked in the kitchen and picked up the kettle of hot water.

Before I knew what was happening, Lydia had emptied the kettle of scalding water over both of my hands.

 I screamed and screamed! "Mama! Mama!" I ran to Mama's bed.

"Lydia! Come here!" Papa shouted. "Young lady, that was an evil thing to do to your sister. All of Ethel's pranks were harmless. I know you get afraid of worms and bugs...and from this day on...Ethel, Frank, and Ema, you are never to tease Lydia again!"

Then, being sorry for scaring Lydia, I thought Papa was just going to forget what she did to me. But, as Mama was greasing my hands with lard and pulling socks over them, Papa said, "And, Lydia, nothing justifies what you have done to Ethel. So, Lydia, you will get up an hour early each morning on school days to fix breakfast and wash the dishes…and go to bed after you have helped with supper and washed the supper dishes…until Ethel's hands are healed."

I wore the socks on my greased-hands for over a month. I asked Lydia to forgive me for scaring her…She asked me to forgive her for burning my hands. And…she did the dishes alone 'til my hands healed. [Papa was a wise man. He taught us to forgive…but, he also taught us, for each wrong action there are consequences.]

Lydia and I became closer during that month. I understood how wrong it was to scare her…she understood how much she should appreciate how hard I work.

After my hands were well, Lydia continued to help with the dishes. And, I made sure Frank never chased her with live worms, again.

Lydia's next birthday will be a better day because we will be better sisters.

Chapter 8:

Mama 'In The Family Way'

"Good morning Dr. McCollum," I greeted as the doctor came in just as we finished breakfast on a cool March mornin'.

"Good mornin', Miss Ethel…Jackson and kids. How 'bout a cup of coffee for a tired Doc," he said as Papa rose from the table.

"Ethel, you fix Dr. McCollum's coffee while we go check your Mama," Papa said.

Papa and Dr. McCollum walked into Mama's bedroom. "Good mornin', Flora," the Doc

said. "How are you feelin' this mornin'?
Have you had much pain lately?"

"Mornin', doc," Mama answered. "I been
painin' some. But…the pains' are not what
I'm worryin' about."

"Well, what's worryin' you, then."

"I believe I'm 'in the family way', Doc," Mama
said.

When Mama said that, I heard
Papa say in a whispered, doubtin'
tone… "No…Flora?"

"Well, we'll just see about that," the Doc
said.

Papa closed the bedroom door behind him
and sat down at the kitchen table. He drank
the coffee I had fixed for the Doc and stared
at the wall. He seemed upset…but said
nothin'.

 Frank called from outside the
kitchen window, "Hey, 'sith',
come 'hep' us 'burry' the dead
baby 'chicknen'."

So, to keep him from botherin' Papa, I went outside. Frank was holdin' the baby chick in his hands. "Let's go to the 'thrine threes'," Frank said, meanin' the 'pine trees' where he and Ema always played. [Too bad Lydia was at school…she would have enjoyed this.]

Back to the burial…Ema cried, actin' like the chick was her only child, "Oh, No…not my baby!"

I was hopin' Mama didn't hear, 'cause it would make her think of Paul.

We got to the pine trees and me and Ema sat down on the ground. Frank placed the chick carefully at his feet—stepped back—and began to preach the funeral.

 " 'Dist' departed one 'est' 'bettur' off than 'usuns'. 'Dist' was a good 'chicknen' and never hurt 'nobidies'," he shouted, firmly. "But, remember, we 'mus' all 'hast' to die and meets our maker. So, you 'bes' be 'saved' 'afore' you die!"

After those partin' words, we all pitched in and dug a tiny 'grave' with our fingers. Then, we placed some pretty leaves over the 'hump'. Frank said a prayer, and the burial was over.

"ETHEL!" Papa hollered from the house. I ran as fast as I could and hollered back for Ema and Frank to go wash their hands in the spring—and bring back a bucket of water to the house for me to wash.

"Yes, Papa," I said barely able to breathe from runnin'.

"Ethel, the Doc just left. He told us we're goin' to have a new baby," Papa said, kinda' happy but kinda' sad at the same time.

 "Oh, Papa, that's wonderful!" I said, grabbin' Papa around the waist.

"It would be wonderful if your Mama was well. But—you know your Mama is real sick," Papa said, hidin' his eyes with his hand. "We're goin' to have to take the best care, ever, of your Mama from now on. If your Mama's sleepin', don't wake her up to ask her nothin'—come ask me. She must have plenty of rest until the baby comes."

"O.K., Papa," I said. "I'll take the best care of Mama. Maybe she'll get well soon."

When I said that, Papa kinda' choked back tears and went outside in a hurry…so I wouldn't see him cry.

That night we all knelt beside our bed after Papa read the Bible. Papa asked me to lead the prayer. "Dear Lord, thank you for dyin' for me. Thank you for our food, for this good house, and for the cool spring where we get our clean water. Thank you for the Doc who takes care of Mama. Thank you for Grandpa and Grandma Bagwell…and please help their corn mill not to break down this summer."

Then I focused on the family… "Now God Bless Frank, Ema, and Lydia. And God Bless Molly and our cow and our chickens and our new hog. And…may the baby chick rest in peace." I knew that would make Frank sleep better.

"And, God, especially Bless Papa, 'cause we love him and he works so hard for us." Then, tryin' not to cry, I said, "And, Lord, please Bless Mama. We sure would love for her to get well and get out of bed again, if it's Your Will, Lord."

Then I concluded, "Well, good night, Lord. We'll be seein' you in the mornin'. Keep us safe tonight, please. And help us to get a good rest."

And we all said, "Amen."

Chapter 9:

The Day Roy Was Born

The summer seemed to fly by and it was now October. I had my eleventh birthday on June 2nd of the year of 1894—Ema started to school—and, Grandpa Bagwell's corn mill didn't break down. But—Mama's still sick.

The Doc came to be with Mama. Friends and neighbors came to the house when they saw the Doc pass their house. They knew it must be time for the new baby to be born.

Even Mrs. Thomas, our neighbor, is here. I don't know if Mama would like that, cause Lydia caught the lice from her two girls........

The Thomas girls came over to play one

day before Mama got sick. The 'lice' was goin' around and Mama told us girls to keep our hair greased good with 'caster oil'. I didn't get 'em, cause I kept my hair greased thick--and Ema's, too.

But…Lydia…didn't want her hair greased. So—before she knew it, she was so 'lousie' that her hair stuck together with 'lice matts' [eggs]. Mama almost had to shave her head to get rid of 'em........

….My mind was shocked back to the present when I heard the cry of a baby.

"It's a fine boy," the Doc said, "and Flora's fine, too."

 Papa came out of the bedroom and thanked everyone for coming and asked them to continue to pray for Mama to be well. Then Grandma Bagwell came out, holdin' the baby. Grandma and some of the other women washed him.

"Papa, can I go in and see Mama?" I asked, hopin' I could.

"O.K., Ethel. But, just for a minute."

I slowly opened the bedroom door and tip-toed inside. "Come here, Ethel," Mama barely whispered when she saw me.

I walked to the bed and Mama held out her hand for mine. "Mama, are you alright?"

"Yes, Ethel, dear…I'm alright. Did they tell you the baby's name?" she asked.

"No, Mama…what is it?"

"We're goin' to name him Roy. Do you like that name, Ethel?

"Oh, yes, Mama…I really like that name."

Then Mama slowly closed her eyes and went to sleep. As I held her hand, I noticed how she had changed in the last year and 8 months. She was kinda' thin and pale…and her hair wasn't as thick—maybe cause she had lay in bed for so long.

Later, I decided while Mama was sleepin', I would iron some clothes. And, then I'll have to start supper while Grandma Bagwell 'tended' to Roy.

"Grandma, can I hold the baby?" I asked, before I go started ironin'.

Grandma gently placed Roy in my arms. When I looked into his tiny eyes, I felt almost as if he were mine…all to myself.

I wondered how God could make such a miracle happen. I thought how Mama must have loved me when I was that little. I  thought how Grandma must have loved Mama when she was that little.

That night…I prayed that Roy wouldn't die like Paul did. I didn't want Mama to be sad. I don't think God did either.

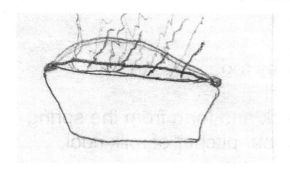

Chapter 10:

Busy, Happy Memories

Change the baby, wash the diapers, feed the baby, change the baby again…my feelin' that I was really Roy's Mama wasn't too far-fetched. I guess I know as much about takin' care of babies as any Mama.

Roy would soon be four months old…the next month in January…and, ever since he was born my life had never been the same. I just thought I had it hard until a baby was added to all the work.

But…he sure was sweet.

Little babies sleep a lot, but they sure let you know when they're hungry. Since Mama was too sick to nurse, I'd  have to run back and forth from the spring where we kept our pitcher of milk cool.

[We would tie the handle to the sealed pitcher to a small tree on the bank of the stream. Then, we would place the pitcher inside the cold water to keep it fresh.]

I would pull up the pitcher and pour some in a pan…run back to the house and heat it for Roy to drink. One of the neighbors rigged-up a 'sort-of' baby bottle for me. My favorite time with Roy was when I held him while he drank milk from the bottle.

I told Grandma Bagwell that I'd be glad when summer comes so Roy would be walkin'. She said I would really have trouble then. She said a walkin' baby is like a young bull let loose in the house—you never know which way they are goin' or what they are goin' to break next.

While I was feedin' Roy, Mama called me... "Ethel."

"Yes, Mama," I said runnin' to the bedroom.

"Put Roy beside me and fetch me some spring water, please, honey."

"O.K., Mama." Mama loved to drink the water from the spring. This bein' December, I have to crack the ice in some places to dip a bucket into the water.

As I bundled-up and ran toward the spring, I saw Papa and the kids comin' thru' the woods. They had walked to Grandma and Grandpa Bagwell's house to tell them we were comin' over on Christmas Eve Night. And...tell them that we will stay for Christmas Dinner.

"Hey, 'sith'," Frank hollered, "where 'ya goin'?"

"I'm goin' to the spring to get Mama some water," I shouted.

Papa waved his hand as if to say… 'take your time…I'll be with your Mama'.

Ema ran to meet me. We slowly walked to the spring. "Ain't Christmas wonderful," she said, as we skipped along, together.

"Do you know what Christmas really means, Ema?" I asked, wondering if she really did.

"Sure, I do," she said. "It's when we remember Jesus was born and have a big, special birthday dinner. You know," she stopped walkin', "we should bake him a cake."

I laughed…and…she got mad.

We got to the spring and Ema helped me get the water for Mama.

As we walked slowly back to the house, we could smell the wood burnin' in the fireplace. All the trees looked like sticks put together, without their leaves.

I was always happy to be outside, walkin' in the pines. That fresh, clean smell of pines kind'a lifts any worries from your mind.

When I was inside, I'd have to work…and…think about Mama's sickness. When I was outside the house, I was in a fresh, beautiful, happy world…no worries.

Papa always said there was nothin' more beautiful than the Georgia hills. And, we lived just enough north of Atlanta to be surrounded by those hills.

In the spring the hills were covered with wild flowers of all colors…in the fall some trees had leaves of many different colors and looked like giant flowers…and, in winter, the leaves are gone—so, you can see for miles and miles.

I remember how Mama used to play outside with us when it snowed. Papa would take some scrap wood and wax the bottom with soap. He'd bore a hole in one side of the square board for a rope. Then he'd pull Mama and us kids all around. The most fun was when he'd push us down the hill toward the spring. We'd have to roll off the board just at the right time to keep from barrellin' into the spring.

Ah…those were wonderful days…when Mama was well.

Chapter 11:

Christmas

Christmas Eve, 1894, finally arrived.

 "Alright, you girls get everything read to go to Grandpa's," Papa said. "Frank, you can watch me put out the fire."

Me, Lydia, and Ema got our gowns and a quilt apiece, since we'd have to sleep on the floor at Grandpa's.

"O. K., Ethel, hitch up Molly while me and the 'younguns' finish up here," Papa said. I couldn't wait 'til Frank was older so he could help with the hitchin'.

Away I ran to get Molly out of the barn. I told our cow I was sorry she'd have to spend Christmas Eve alone. But...I reminded her to kneel and pray at midnight. [That was an old country tradition at Christmas for cows, Mama told us.]

I walked Molly toward the house where Papa had left the wagon. By that time Lydia and Ema were coming out the door with their arms loaded, headed for the wagon.

After steadying Molly, I helped Lydia and Ema fix a pallet for Mama in the back of the wagon.

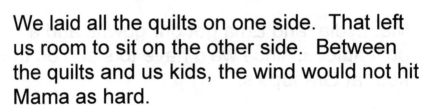

We laid all the quilts on one side. That left us room to sit on the other side. Between the quilts and us kids, the wind would not hit Mama as hard.

Papa carried Mama out the door with Frank toddlein' behind. "Go get Roy," Papa said.

Roy was bundled up like a tiny Eskimo. I lifted him off the bed and slowly walked to the wagon. "This is nice, girls," Mama said, as Papa helped her get comfortable on the pallet of quilts we had made. I laid Roy beside her. She turned on her side and cuddled him with her arms.

"O.K., jump in," Papa told Ema, Frank and Lydia. Then me and Papa hooked Molly to the wagon.

We rode slow so Mama wouldn't get bumped. "You O.K., Flora?" Papa said.

"Yes, fine. It's wonderful to be outside again," she said.

" 'Sanna Caus' comin' tonight. Ain't he Ma?" Frank sputtered.

"Well, son," Mama said, "you just be thankful now for whatever gifts you get." Mama loved surprising us on Christmas morning

59

with gifts…she never really said where they came from.

"Oh, 'yeth', Ma…I 'weill'…I 'willy weill'," Frank said…crossing his heart.

We arrived at Grandpa's and got Mama settled on the bed and Molly in the barn. Aunt Tampi, Mama's sister, and her girl, Mamie, were there.

Tampi and Mamie stayed at Grandpa's off and on, 'cause Aunt Tampi's husband drank a lot and got drunk sometimes. They were afraid of him when he was on a drunk.

We all talked and played after we ate a bite of supper. Then, Papa hung our stockings over the fireplace. Frank was worried that his stockin' was too small. Grandma told Frank not to worry. Ema, being the perfect sister, was just having a great time, playing with Mamie. Ema hardly, ever got upset or was jealous of anybody else.

Papa read the scriptural account of Jesus' Birth. He explained that He was born to pay the price for our sins. That all of us must pray for Jesus to come into our hearts. And, when we sincerely ask for forgiveness when we feel we have done wrong, Jesus will help us to not do any bad thing again.

 [Of course, Papa used simple terms to explain the 'New Birth' to us kids. I, being the oldest, knew and understood more…especially since I had already prayed and accepted Jesus as my Savior.]

Mama cautioned us that God sees everything we do, and that Jesus is in heaven defending us until we pray for forgiveness for ourselves. Grandma reminded us it is always best not to do wrong, 'cause, even 'tho we may be forgiven when we pray, we still must face the 'consequences' of our wrong doin'.

 Grandpa said, "Yeah…just like that young boy who robbed a store. He can get forgiveness from God

for his sin of robbing the store…but…he will still go to jail for his sin."

 Wow! That puts a lot more focus on doing right.

"Alright, you younguns', you best go to sleep. The morning will get here fast enough to see what surprise is under the tree with your name on it," Grandma said. She also explained that we give gifts to each other as a token of our love for each other— just like the 'three kings' gave gifts to Jesus after his Birth.

After we all got settled in our quilt pallets on the floor, we were cozy warm, lying in front of the fireplace. It was a happy, safe feeling—seeing the stockings…watching the fire…and looking around the room, knowing we would all be so excited in the mornin'.

 It seemed I had just closed my eyes when I heard feet shuffling on the floor near the fireplace. It was

Grandpa, putting logs on the fire. The fire had almost gone out during the night.

Frank woke up and ran toward the tree, steppin' on my stomach and Lydia's leg—then he fell on top of Ema. By this time, and with Frank's injurin' all us kids, everybody was awake. Papa lit the lamp so we could see around the room better.

We each took down our stockin' and looked inside. We got some raisins, some candy, and a little China Doll each…even Frank. We all just loved our dolls, 'cause we had always wanted one.

"Oh…look what I got!" Mamie shouted from the back of the kitchen. On the kitchen table was some beautiful material for a new dress and some new 'store-bought' shoes, with her stockin' laying across them—showin' they were hers.

At first, I got real hurt. I didn't understand why she got so much, 'cause I knew I worked lots harder than Mamie ever did. Then, I figured maybe it was 'cause she didn't have a good Papa.

Maybe the Lord worked it out to give her more 'things', since she has less of the stuff that really counts.

I realized I'd rather have my good Papa than a hundred new dresses. That's what I whispered to Lydia, Ema, and Frank—and, they agreed.

So, bein' thankful for what we got and what we have always had, us kids spent a wonderful Christmas Day—eatin', laughin', and playin' with our new dolls.

Chapter 12:

The End and
The Beginning

Grandma and Grandpa Burgess had come to stay with us a while since last Sunday after church. They didn't live very far away, but they didn't get to visit much.

Us girls thought Grandpa Burgess was too jealous of Grandma 'cause he made her wear a bonnet in public to hide her face from men.

Papa's sister, Mary Wills, was already staying with us since Christmas, so that

Grandma Bagwell could stay home for a while. It had only been a couple of weeks since we spent Christmas at Grandma and Grandpa Bagwell's house.

 I got up that mornin' as usual and started breakfast. Bein' the middle of January, the weather was cold and it had started snowin' outside.

I saw the Doc comin' and met him at the door. He was comin' by a lot the last few months, checkin' on Mama.

"Mornin', Ethel," he said.

"Mornin', Doc," I answered.

"How's your Ma today?"

"Pretty good. Aunt Mary is still stayin' with us. They been laughin' and talkin' this mornin'."

While I settled the kids around the table, the Doc went in the bedroom to see Mama.

Later, after we had finished eatin', I was washin' the dishes. The younguns' were playin' outside in the snow—when—all of a sudden, Papa came burstin' out of the bedroom. He grabbed his coat and ran out of the house.

I ran in to see Mama.

She smiled at me and said, "Ethel, iron me a clean gown, please, honey."

I didn't understand why, but it seemed just a few minutes when Grandpa and Grandma Bagwell arrived. Then the neighbors started coming in. They all just stood around in the kitchen with Grandma and Grandpa Burgess and kept whisperin' to each other.

I pushed my way into the bedroom to see what was happenin'. The Doc had been in there a long time. Just as I walked in, Mama said to Aunt Mary, "I can't see my way clear as I should." Aunt Mary called the Doc over to the bed.

Mama took the Doc's hand and said, "Is there anything else you can do for me, Doc?"

The Doc took a deep breath and shook his head, "No, Flora, I've done all I can. The sickness is in your lungs. The medicine doesn't seem to be helping."

"Well," Mama said with a big gasp, "God Bless you—meet me in heaven."

Then Mama asked for all the family to come close to the bed. I then realized what was happenin'.

"Mama, Mama," I said, holdin' back tears, as I ran to the bed and hugged Mama around the neck.

Mama held my hands and with a sweet smile, she said, "Ethel, honey, you go get your Mama some of that good, cold spring water—and hurry up, now."

I passed Frank, Ema, and Lydia as they were comin' inside from the snow, grabbin' my coat and the water pail. I ran as fast as I could, not mindin' the cold or snow. I reached the spring... broke the thin ice on the water... and, scooped down in the spring with the pail.

By now I was cryin' so hard, I could barely see the house thru' my tears, as I ran home.

I rushed in the house and headed for the bedroom.

Everyone was huggin' each other and cryin'. Papa was holdin' Mama in his arms and cryin' like I never heard before. Different neighbors were holdin' Lydia, Ema, Frank, and Roy.

 My heart sunk. I walked over to Grandpa Bagwell and said, "But I brought the spring water as fast as I could, Grandpa."

Grandpa Bagwell looked down at me, and said, "It's too late, Ethel. She's almost gone."

I stood in shock for a few seconds, not wanting to believe what Grandpa said.

Then, I dropped the pail and grabbed Grandpa Bagwell around the legs…and cried and cried.

I glanced back at Mama. She opened her eyes and looked around the room…then her eyes fixed on me, and she said… "I love you all…goodbye…meet me in heaven."

Then, her breathing stopped, and Mama went to heaven.

Papa fell back and laid out on the floor. I started to scream—'cause I thought Papa was dead, too.

The next thing I remembered, I was in the church. I saw the pine box at the front of the church and I knew Mama was in it. What we had dreaded for two years, ever since Mama got sick, was finally here.

As I sat there durin' the service, I could hear Mama's voice as she would tell me, "You're the Mama, now, Ethel… 'cause Mama's too sick'. But I'll teach you all you need to now—you'll do fine."   …The End

EPILOG

Just like Mama said, I raised all the younguns' 'just fine'. Lydia and Ema became teachers—in school and at church. Frank was always an outstanding business man and well known in the community of Alpharetta, Georgia. Roy owned a store between Roswell and Norcross, Georgia, near the Chattahoochee River.

I married Early Royston Nalley, January 4th, 1906. He died of a stroke on October 14th, 1931. Early and I had seven children: Quentine, Annis, Jarrell, Glenn, Emory, Frank and Marshall.

Glenn died a few months after birth. Jarrell died November 12th, 1968. Quintine died on May 24th, 1976. My only daughter, Annis [Carol's mother], died July 26th, 1977. My youngest, Marshall, died December 8th, 1979. [Frank died in early '80s.]

I have great-great grandchildren I've never seen. I lived longer than any of my brothers and sisters. As of the year 1980, I, Ethel Burgess-Nalley, am 96 years old.

<u>From the Author</u>:

My Grandma died in February of 1981.

Grandma Nalley was the sweetest, wisest, prettiest woman I have ever known. Her time of council and love are always a part of me.

Here is a photo taken when my Mama was only about 2 or 3 years old…she's sitting in Grandma's lap.

<u>Back row</u>…left to right: Roy and Frank, **Grandma's brothers**; Jackson's 2nd wife; Ema, **Grandma's sister [not sure who the 2 children in front of her are…could be her children or Jackson's step-children].**

<u>Middle row</u>…left to right: my Grandpa, Early Nalley;
       my Grandma, Ethel Burgess-Nalley;
       my Great-Grandpa, Jackson Burgess.

<u>Front row</u>…left to right: Quentine, Annis [my Mama], and grandma's half brother, Curtis.